W9-BJD-699

Fur-Ever Yours, Booker Jones

Duffey, Betsy

Lex: 440 R.L: 4.3   GRL: Pts: 5

There was a knock on the door.

Booker's mother came in. Something was different about her. As a writer, Booker prided himself on noticing things about people. Mrs. Brite, his creative writing teacher, always told the class, "Think details." He looked at his mother and tried to tell what was different. Aha! It was her hair: it was redder. It was poofier.

"Booker, Libba's going to take over the cooking this week, and you're going to be responsible for the laundry," his mother said.

Laundry? He had never done laundry before. There were dirty clothes everywhere. There was a pile by his bed, another by his closet, another beside the door, and that was just his own room. It was like a horror story:

It came in the darkness of night, first one sock then two. Dirty underwear and T-shirts creeping toward him. "Wash us," they whispered.

"Booker, are you listening?" His head snapped up and he nodded.

"Laundry," he said.

"[A] fast-paced, varied, and often touching story. . . .A fine choice [for] young writers."   —*Kirkus Reviews*

ALSO BY BETSY DUFFEY

Fur-ever Yours, Booker Jones

Betsy Duffey

PUFFIN BOOKS

PUFFIN BOOKS
Published by the Penguin Group
Penguin Putnam Books for Young Readers,
345 Hudson Street, New York, New York 10014, U.S.A.
Penguin Books Ltd, 80 Strand, London WC2R ORL, England
Penguin Books Australia Ltd, 250 Camberwell Road, Camberwell, Victoria 3124, Australia
Penguin Books Canada Ltd, 10 Alcorn Avenue, Toronto, Ontario, Canada M4V 3B2
Penguin Books (N.Z.) Ltd, 182-190 Wairau Road, Auckland 10, New Zealand

Penguin Books Ltd, Registered Offices: Harmondsworth, Middlesex, England

First published in the United States of America by Viking,
a division of Penguin Putnam Books for Young Readers, 2001
Published by Puffin Books,
a division of Penguin Putnam Books for Young Readers, 2002

1 3 5 7 9 10 8 6 4 2

THE LIBRARY OF CONGRESS HAS CATALOGED THE VIKING EDITION AS FOLLOWS:
Duffey, Betsy.
Fur-ever yours, Booker Jones / Betsy Duffey.
p. cm.
Summary: Twelve-year-old Booker Jones turns to his writing once again
to deal with the stress of his parents' decision to vacation
together, leaving family and laundry behind.
ISBN 0-670-89287-4 (hardcover)
[1. Authorship—Fiction. 2. Grandfathers—Fiction. 3. Brothers and sisters—Fiction.
4. Schools—Fiction. 5. Family life—Fiction.] I. Title.
PZ7.D876 Fu 2001
[Fic]—dc21
2001000439

Puffin Books ISBN 0-14-230215-5

Printed in the United States of America

For Bobby, Lynn,
and Nancy

CONTENTS

Booker Jones
Pickle Springs, AR

September 15

Hamerstein Books
New York, NY

Dear Editor,

I am writing about my new book, <u>Monstroid</u>.

There's this kid, and he gets a new computer and he's playing a space game called Monstroid. He accidentally punches ENTER and he enters the computer! He hears a beeping noise . . . he turns slowly . . . he's face-to-face with . . . MONSTROID!

Will someone press ESCAPE so he can get out? Will they press it in time? Read the exciting <u>Monstroid</u> to find the answers.

When I sent you my book <u>Space Cows</u> you said that it did not meet the needs of your list. Will <u>Monstroid</u> meet the needs of your list? What are the needs of your list? What is a list?

Expectantly yours,

Booker Jones

Booker Jones
Pickle Springs, AR

September 18

Hamerstein Books
New York, NY

Dear Editor,

Here is my sequel to <u>Monstroid</u>. I call it <u>Monstroid II</u>. I went ahead and started it even though you have not had time to read <u>Monstroid I</u>. I couldn't help myself.

See, the boy does get out of the computer. His mother accidentally punches ESCAPE while dusting and the boy escapes but . . . <u>Monstroid escapes with him</u>!!!

Here's the first line: <u>Todd stared at the computer screen—from the inside</u>! Here's the last line: <u>Monstroid became smaller and smaller, pixel by pixel, until he was a tiny glowing spot on the computer screen. "Good-bye reality," he called as he disappeared. "I will return."</u> Between those two sentences—over two thousand perfect words. Here it is, see for yourself.

Anxiously Yours,

Booker Jones

(1)

Crash Position

Citizens of Pickle Springs, Arkansas, Red Alert! Sistoid has entered the town and has seized control of a vehicle of destruction. Take shelter immediately. Clear the streets. Run for your lives. . . .

Booker hunched over in the back seat of his father's Chevy, his head tucked between his legs for safety. His sister, Libba, was having a driving lesson and he wanted to be prepared. He had come along to collect data—true-life experiences were vital to his writing. So far, the lesson had not disappointed him.

"Hey." He looked up into the front seat. Libba's pink-ribboned ponytail was swaying with the movement of the car. "What's crash position?"

"Dad," Libba whined from the driver's seat. "Make him stop."

"Booker," his father said in a tight voice.

"I'm serious," Booker said, sitting up. "I know you put your head down, but do your arms go over your head or around your knees?"

The car lurched to the left and horns blared. A man in a blue pickup shook his fist.

As he was thrown hard, once to the left, then immediately back to the right, Booker flung his arms wide across the back seat of the car for support. His notebook slid from his lap to the floor.

"Slow down! Slow down!" His father, who was usually so quiet and calm, was red-faced and excited.

The old Chevy jerked forward then came to a sudden halt that snapped Booker's head back. The term whiplash took on new meaning for him: his neck had made the exact motion of a lion-tamer's whip.

"Take it easy, Libba," his father said. "This car is like a gun in your hand. It's dangerous."

"You are just making me nervous," Libba said. "I don't like it when you yell at m—"

But the rest was lost in a roar as Libba floored it and they charged once more into traffic.

Sistoid terrorized the town of Pickle Springs with her vehicle of destruction. She rolled over small houses and a few cats. Grinning evilly, she gripped the controls. "I will annihilate the world!" she called as she turned toward Little Rock.

"Easy, easy." His father pressed his body against the

passenger door as if he might open it and jump out at any moment.

In the side mirror Booker could see his father's wide eyes. They reminded him of a panicked wombat he had seen on *Animal Kingdom,* right before the wombat had been devoured by a large Australian snake.

It was the kind of detail he would normally have written down in his notebook. Right now it was much too dangerous to write.

As they made their way down Main Street, Booker looked out the window hoping to see his best friend Germ or some of the other guys from school. Maybe he could get Libba to let him out.

"Turn right," his father said in a tense voice.

Libba waved to some girls coming out of the video store and honked the horn.

"Pay attention, Libba. Now, turn," he said louder. Then louder still, *"Turn!"*

All at once the car bumped up onto the curb and veered toward the Dairy Queen. A lady with a stroller screamed and leapt back, yanking the stroller with her. A cat froze against the wall, its eyes bulging with fear, fur standing straight up. Booker got into crash position.

"Whoaaaa!" his father yelled like a cowboy.

Just in time, the car stopped. Booker looked up to see his father reach over and turn the key.

Silence.

"You told me to turn," Libba said.

His father sat stunned, the car keys in one hand, the other hand on his heart as though he might recite the Pledge of Allegiance.

"You almost killed that woman," he said finally. He threw his hands in the air in a gesture of defeat. "And a cat."

Libba was taking deep breaths now—the kind that signal tears.

"I . . . was . . . just . . ."

"I think I remember now," Booker said, rubbing his forehead.

"What?" his father asked.

"What crash position is."

"One more crack like that and you can walk home!" His father's voice got louder and louder.

Booker sat back and vowed never to speak again, like the monks who live in the mountains of Tibet.

Lately he never quite knew what to say. His father's moods had become so unpredictable. Booker was pretty sure it had something to do with a book that he had discovered on his father's bedside table, *30 Days to a More Incredible Marriage*. His parents, who were usually so normal, had become so *strange*. Last month, he had looked outside and seen them jumping on a trampoline together. Two weeks ago his father had appeared at dinner wearing a new wetsuit and snorkel and announced that he was taking scuba lessons. Tomorrow they were leaving on a trip to Mexico.

It was like a story Booker was working on about a brain mix-up gun that changed people by confusing their thoughts. In his head, he wrote a new episode:

The brain mix-up gun was on. The safety had released and the dangerous mix-up rays were aimed at the boy's parents. It fired! Instantly, thoughts of work and responsibility were replaced with thoughts of trampolines and wetsuits. The man spoke: "We're going to Mexico."

"Well, that was just great," Booker's father said. Libba blew her nose.

"It's only . . . my third . . . lesson," she said tearfully.

His father closed his eyes and laid his head back against the headrest.

People on the sidewalk stepped around the car, peering curiously through the windows as they passed.

Booker retrieved his notebook and thought for a moment. An image of lurching and swerving teased his brain—that kind of out-of-control feeling you have on a roller coaster or on a water slide or when your teacher announces a pop quiz. In the middle of it all, he kept picturing the cat, eyes wide, frozen in fear.

He began to write.

The ship plunged through outer space, tossing and turning like a glowing red rock spewed from a volcano. The kitten assumed crash position to avoid whiplash as the ship alternated between sudden starts and stops. He was deafened by a rumbling roar around the ship.

A new book had begun. Booker breathed a deep sigh of satisfaction—a creator breathing life into his new creation. Already there were important questions forming in his mind.

What was happening? Why was the ship out of control? Was there any hope for the kitten? What was the rumbling roar? Was "rumbling roar around" too many *r*s in one sentence?

"Let's go home," his father said finally, opening the car door. He signaled people to step back, then walked around to the driver's side. Libba scooted over to the passenger seat. The car started and they eased off the curb, then moved forward. No one spoke.

(2)

Blast Off!

Booker sat at his desk after dinner, listening to the hum of his typewriter. His friends always asked why he didn't use a computer, but this old machine had a history that no computer would ever have. On this typewriter Booker's grandfather had written more than one hundred newspaper columns, and Booker had written five of his own novels.

A stack of white paper sat beside him, just waiting to be filled up with words. Booker rolled in a clean sheet and rested his chin on his hands.

This was the happiest part of writing a book. The idea was fresh in his mind—the images clear. The paragraph he had written in the car would come later in the book. Now he would go back to how it all began.

He looked around his room as he thought. It hadn't always been his bedroom. His parents had converted the dining room into a bedroom for him after Pop, his grandfather, had moved in with them.

There was a knock on the door and his mother came

in. "We're just packing the last things," she said in an excited voice. "Do you have a fanny pack?"

Something was different about his mother. As a writer, Booker prided himself on noticing things about people. Mrs. Brite, his creative writing teacher, always told the class, "Think details." He looked at his mother and tried to tell what was different. Aha! It was her hair: It was redder. It was *poofier*. She opened the top drawer of his dresser.

"I don't have one," he answered.

"Booker, Libba's going to take over the cooking while we are gone and you're going to be responsible for the laundry," she said. She closed the drawer then patted her hair as she studied her reflection in the mirror over his dresser.

Laundry? He had never done laundry before. There were dirty clothes everywhere. There was a pile by his bed, another by his closet, another beside the door, and that was just his own room. It was like a horror story.

It came in the darkness of night, first one sock then two. Dirty underwear and T-shirts creeping toward him. "Wash us," they whispered.

"Booker, are you listening?" His head snapped up and he nodded.

"Laundry," he said to show he understood. "Mom?" he asked.

"Yes?"

"Do you really think that it's a good idea, going to Mexico?"

"What do you mean?" Her eyes narrowed and her hand stopped patting.

"Well . . . leaving us alone."

She frowned. "You're not alone," she said. "You have Libba and Pop. You sound like you don't want us to go. Don't you want your dad and me to have some fun?"

He didn't answer. The answer was "no" but it sounded so selfish. How could he tell her that he actually *wanted* them to be home, acting normal and taking care of him?

"We all need to think of others, Booker."

His kindergarten teacher, Mrs. Williams, used to say things like that.

"It's time for you to grow up," his mother continued.

Booker's mouth fell open. It was bad enough that his parents were leaving but now they wanted him to grow up, too?

"*La cucaracha! La cucaracha!*" His father came into the room and started dancing around in a Mexican hat. Obviously the stress of the driving lesson was forgotten.

His mother laughed and joined in. As they danced out together, Booker remembered the cat's face when Libba almost ran him over. He felt the same stunned look come over his own face as he watched their pathetic dancing.

Things were moving too fast and there was nothing that he could do to stop it. Booker shook his head to clear his mind.

Ideas for his new book began to bubble up inside of him. It was like the bubbles in a Coke that you drink too fast, painful until you burp it out. He typed.

Chapter One

Meow!

There was a soft meow from the interior of the space capsule as it sat on the launch ramp.

Meow!

Louder this time as strange noises came from the control panel.

The kitten was confused. Only moments before he had been nestled in the control room, where he had discovered a new place to sleep—a warm pile of packing material.

Then there had been chaotic motion, a random jerking. He had been dumped with the packing material into the nose cone!

Back at mission control, the countdown began.

Twenty . . .

Nineteen . . .

Eighteen . . .

"Where's the cat?"

"What cat?"

"The one that was right under here, by my feet."

"Pay attention. We're T minus fifteen seconds."

Fourteen . . .

Thirteen . . .

"Here, kitty, kitty."

"I told you not to bring that cat in here."

"He's just a kitten. How far could he go?"

Eleven . . .

Ten . . .

"That cat is here somewhere."

"Hey, concentrate on the mission. We'll find the cat later."

Meow!

The kitten hunkered down, trembling, as the booster engines ignited, roaring loudly.

Three . . .

Two . . .

One . . .

Meow!

Blast off!

The small cat unwillingly began his journey.

(3)

Alone in Space

Booker tapped the ends of his pages to even them out. He selected a green paper clip and clipped them together. His first chapter was complete. He thought about reading it to Pop, who was the one person in the house who appreciated his stories.

Booker walked down the hall to Pop's room and paused by his sister's door. She was laughing into the telephone, recounting the driving lesson.

"Then . . . Then . . . Then . . ." Libba was laughing so hard she couldn't get the words out. "Then we bumped up on the curb in front of the Dairy Queen. Mrs. Nelson was there, you know from seventh grade English . . . Right! Gerunds!"

He leaned back against the wall and listened. If he hadn't been present he would never have believed it was the same experience. There was no mention of the whiplash he had suffered, or the car horns and screeching tires. Just last week in creative writing class they had learned about point of view, the same event told from different perspectives:

Libba: It was sooooo cool. I was sooooo in control. It was, like, sooooo neat. There is nothing to it. I mean nothing.

Mrs. Nelson: I saw the car coming at me and my life flashed before my eyes. All those participles left dangling forever.

Dad: If she would only pay attention. A car is like a gun in a teenager's hand. These kids. These kids.

The Dairy Queen Man: I'll never forget, it was a chocolate vanilla swirl. I had just put the curlicue on the top when it happened. I heard a screech that sent a chill down my spine. I saw the car coming and I said to myself, "This is the last cone for me."

Cat: Me-ow!

He peeked in and saw Libba pick up a nail file and begin to saw on a perfect oval fingernail. It reminded Booker of a claw. No, a *talon.* He would make a note of it for one of his books.

"Mo-om!" Libba yelled. "Booker's spying on me."

"Right!" he called into the room, "like I want to be bored to death."

"You kids stop fighting," his mother called from her bedroom. "We don't have time for that."

He moved on down the hall and stopped by Pop's door. Pop was sitting at his desk leaning over an old book. Lamplight illuminated his face as he concentrated on the pages in front of him. He wore the same gray sweater and leather slippers that he had worn for years. The light made him look even older and more fragile than he was.

"Pop?"

"Come in," Pop said.

Booker stepped into the room. He could never walk into his old room without feeling the memories there, the stories that he had written at the very desk where Pop was sitting.

"What's that?" he asked, pointing at the book.

"A journal," Pop said. "Memories." He leaned back in the chair and stretched his shoulders. Booker looked down at one of the pages. It was yellow and brown around the edges but the writing was bold and black. Pop's hand trembled as he turned the pages.

"It's pretty old," Booker said.

"I'm pretty old," Pop answered, pushing his reading glasses up on his nose.

Booker watched as Pop leafed through the book until he came to a place where a purple violet was pressed between the pages.

The flower was still a brilliant purple even though it was dried and stiff. "This came from the river," Pop said. "I put it in here so I wouldn't forget the day I picked it."

"What day was that Pop?"

Pop shrugged. "Don't know," he said. "Now I have to read to see what I did."

"May I read it?"

Pop nodded.

Booker read over Pop's shoulder. It was about his grandmother.

We sat by the river today. Daisy heard a bobwhite calling. She taught me that—to listen for birds, the call of the whippoorwill, the screech of a jay. She taught me to look for flowers beside the bank. As long as I have lived here, as many times as I have looked at the river, there are things that I have never seen. She shows me. A tiny raccoon print in the sand. A bobwhite. A violet.

I think I'll scatter seed along the yard beside the river to bring the birds close.

Booker looked up from the journal to Pop. "It's nice, Pop," he said. Pop's face was frozen like a statue, his eyes squinted closed. "That is the power of words," Pop said finally.

"What do you mean?" Booker asked.

"The power to hold a moment."

He rested his head in his hands on top of the book.

He had forgotten Booker completely. Booker looked down at the paper-clipped pages of his own story and lost the desire to share them. He watched Pop for a moment then backed quietly out of the room.

In the hall he heard his parents laughing in their room. Libba was on the phone still talking. Pop was silently lost in his memories. In a house full of people, Booker was completely alone.

Booker retreated to his bedroom. He thought about the cat and his feelings: alone. Alone in space! It was the perfect title for his story. He rolled a clean sheet of paper into his typewriter and typed his title page.

Space Cat: Alone in Space

by

Booker Jones

Booker pulled the page out and studied it. Usually this moment felt great—seeing the title typed out for the first time. But this time his new title just made him feel lonely.

Booker Jones
Pickle Springs, AR

September 30

Hamerstein Books
New York, NY

Dear Editor,

    Enclosed is the first chapter of my latest novel . . . <u>Space Cat: Alone in Space!</u> I could not wait to finish the whole book before sending off this first chapter to you.

Purr-fectly yours,
Booker Jones

(4)

All Was Chaos

"We're off!" his mother said cheerfully.

The morning had been a whirlwind of activity. Now a yellow taxi waited out front to pick up his parents.

"Now you'll be okay, won't you?" she asked, gathering up the suitcases in the hall.

"We'll be fine, Mom," Libba said.

Booker wasn't so sure. He still couldn't believe they were leaving.

His mother wore a sundress with a blue straw hat. His father wore a new Hawaiian-print shirt. He carried the suitcases out to the taxi.

"I can't believe we're going!" his mom said for the fiftieth time. "I just can't believe it."

"I hope we're doing the right thing," his father said as he put the suitcases in the trunk.

"We are," his mother said firmly. She turned to Booker and hugged him. "Ask Pop if you need anything."

Booker and Libba waved from the driveway as the taxi pulled away.

"I guess we're on our own," Libba said.

Booker watched the taxi as it rounded the corner and disappeared. "I guess so," he answered.

Booker thought about his father's book and sighed. *30 Days to a More Incredible Marriage.* He had looked the word "incredible" up in his dictionary. It meant unbelievable or extraordinary. It was too hard to understand. He did not like change. Parents should stay the same.

That was one thing Booker loved about Pop: consistency. Pop always wore the same gray sweater, with the same three buttons buttoned down the front. He said the same things and looked the same. It was comforting.

His friend Germ was like that, too. He knew without looking what Germ would wear: jeans and a T-shirt. What he would say: "Hey, Bookworm." What he would do: eat on the way to school. Yes, consistency was good. He liked that in a friend.

He lifted his backpack onto his shoulder and looked one last time at the house. As he waved to Pop, he noticed that something seemed different about him. He couldn't quite decide what it was. Think detail. What was it?

"Come on," Libba yelled. He shrugged and headed to the bus. Booker threw himself at the steps just before the bus pulled out. He swung his backpack down and slid into the seat with Germ.

"Hey, Bookworm," Germ said. He lifted his backpack

onto his lap to make more room for Booker. Booker settled back into the seat with a contented smile. It was good to be away from the house. Libba moved to the back of the bus.

As they bumped along toward school he thought about his mother's poofier, redder hair and his parents' trip. He frowned.

"Did your parents ever act weird?" he asked Germ.

"Of course, they're parents."

"I mean weirder than usual, like changing their hairstyle. Or going to exotic places, like Mexico?"

"Yeah. It even has a name, mid-life crisis. That's what my mother called it."

The bus rumbled on, but Booker's mind stopped abruptly, circling around the word. "Crisis," Booker said. It intrigued him. He opened his backpack and pulled out his pocket dictionary.

Crisis: a stage in a series of events at which the trend of all future events is determined; a turning point.

So far, the series of events in his parents' life included jumping on a trampoline and coming to dinner in a wetsuit. Would the future be determined by these things?

The bus rounded a corner and Booker leaned against Germ then straightened up. "Are you sure that's what it's called?" he asked.

Germ nodded. He balanced his backpack on his knees

as he rifled through it. "All parents get it sooner or later," he said. He pulled out a brown paper bag and a spiral notebook.

"Your parents went through it?" Booker asked.

"Yeah, especially my dad. Remember when he bought that black leather jacket and the matching leather pants?"

"I don't remember," Booker answered.

"It was probably too painful and you blocked it out." Germ unrolled the top of the brown paper bag, looked inside, and made a face. "Tuna fish," he said in a disappointed voice.

"How long did it last?" Booker asked.

"What?"

"The crisis thing."

Germ thought for a moment, then shrugged. "I don't remember. Right in the middle of it I went to camp. Then when I came home everything seemed back to normal." Germ put the notebook on top of his backpack like a table and sorted out the contents of his lunch. Sandwich, chips, dill pickle, and Swiss Cake rolls.

"My parents just left for Mexico," Booker said.

Germ whistled softly, like a tire leaking air. "They got a bad case of it," he said. "My parents only went to the Poconos."

They rode along not speaking as Germ munched his chips.

The bus lurched to the right, then to the left, as it

crossed a speed bump. Paper wads flew through the air. Libba and her friends practiced a cheer in the back of the bus. They stomped and clapped. Two girls sang a song in the front of the bus. All was chaos.

Quickly, Booker pulled his notebook out of his backpack. He had the first line of his next chapter!

He wrote:

All was chaos.

Perfect.

Now what?

Crisis. He liked the idea of putting his cat in a crisis.

If a crisis was a turning point, then his first chapter already had a crisis. His cat was zooming into outer space. An innocent kitten caught in circumstances beyond its control. He continued to write:

The crisis had begun. The small kitten cowered in a corner of the spaceship as it jolted forward. Out of the stratosphere. Darker and darker into deep space.

The men and women at mission control cheered and clapped.

"We have liftoff."

"Hooray!"

"Successful launch!"

"Mars, here we come."

They were oblivious to the fate of the small cat inside the spaceship.

"So. Are you joining?"

"What?" Booker turned his attention back to Germ who had just finished off a Swiss Cake Roll and was licking the paper.

"Joining what?"

"Ha! For once I know something about writing that you don't know." He crumpled the wrapper and put it in his pocket. A bit of chocolate still clung to his lip.

"What about writing?"

"The writing club."

A writing club? Booker was immediately taken with the idea. Many great writers had been in writing groups. Tolkien and C. S. Lewis were in a group together. A writing club could add a whole new dimension to his writing. In all his concern about his parents he had missed something important.

"What writing club?"

"Mrs. Brite is starting a writing club. We're meeting today after school."

"We?" Booker was surprised. He was imagining Tolkien and C.S. Lewis, not Germ Germondo. "You're in it?"

"Sure."

"But you hate to write."

"It meets my criteria for a club."

"You mean they have food."

"Yeah."

"I guess I'll come," Booker said.

"You have to write something to get in," Germ said. He tucked the tuna sandwich back in his pack and opened his notebook. The pages were perfectly clean.

"How are you going to get in?" Booker asked, looking at Germ's spotless notebook.

"I do my best work under pressure," Germ said. He closed his eyes and tapped his pencil on his forehead.

"Hey, I've got my first lines: There once was a teacher named Brite . . . who wanted her students to write." He licked the tip of his pencil. "This writing thing is easier than I thought."

Booker frowned. "I don't think a limerick qualifies as writing."

Germ was not discouraged. He was already jotting the lines down in the spiral notebook.

"I hear she's having brownies," he went on. "She makes this kind with mint icing on top. She calls it Brite's Delight."

Germ scratched his head with the pencil tip, then began writing as he spoke. "So she started a club . . . and brought out some grub."

Booker shook his head.

"One more line . . ."

As the bus bumped along, Booker stared at his own notebook. He could turn this chapter in to the writing club. If he could finish it.

"I got it! I got it!" Germ stood up and yelled. "I, Germ Germondo, poet, have composed a poem." Paper wads hit Germ.

> *"There once was a teacher named Brite*
> *who wanted her students to write.*
> *So she started a club*
> *and brought out some grub.*
> *Now the writers might write for Delight."*

The kids on the bus applauded and cheered. Booker put his pen down and looked at Germ.

While he struggled with words, desperate to come up with just the perfect way to say things, Germ had not only written something but was already receiving applause.

Germ bowed and held his hands out to signal more applause.

What was going on? *He* had always been the writer. *Germ* had always been the audience.

He looked at Germ with new eyes. He didn't like what he saw.

The kitten blinked and looked around the space capsule. Suddenly everything in his life had changed. Where was his water bowl, his feather toy, his litter box?

Where was his scratching post, his catnip mouse, his Little Whiskas?

Where was his owner who fed him and rubbed his back?

Nothing was the same.

The day had started with a series of events that

made it different from others. His parents, usually so boring, were wearing funny clothes on a plane to Mexico. Germ, who had never written a single story that wasn't a class assignment, had received applause for writing. And Pop . . . even Pop had been different. But how? Booker remembered Pop standing at the door as he left. *Think detail,* he told himself. And then he knew what it was: Pop's gray sweater had been inside out.

(5)

Eclipso the Evil

Mrs. Brite was a small woman with a very large mouth. She resembled a Muppet, or the wide-mouthed frog Booker had read about in a picture book when he was little.

But she was talking about writing, so Booker paid attention. This was his favorite class. Mrs. Brite loved books and writing as much as he did.

"Many elements come together to make up a story. Dialogue, plot, setting, point of view. These are just a few of the elements of a story that we'll be learning about."

Booker leaned forward and listened closer.

"Dialogue is just pure speech. The spoken interchange of ideas. Take out a sheet of paper and try writing some dialogue—two people talking to each other. Just their words."

Booker was always pleased when he could combine a writing assignment with his own stories. That way he could write in class without getting into trouble.

He thought for a moment. Slowly the setting and characters of his book drifted into his brain, and the spaceship appeared.

Booker leaned forward and rested the tip of his pencil on the top line for a moment, then began.

At mission control the room was buzzing with activity. A giant screen plotted the trajectory course of the spaceship. People with clipboards hurried back and forth across the white tile floor, gathering and distributing data.

Booker stopped and scratched through the lines— only dialogue, he reminded himself.

He tried again.

"Captain?"

"Yes, General."

"Have you checked the vital readings of the ship?"

"We're in the process of checking them, Sir."

"O2 level?"

"The O2 level is normal, Sir."

"Temperature?"

"Seventy-five degrees. Everything seems normal. But . . ."

"But what? Captain?"

"But there's a strange noise coming from the capsule."

"A noise? Report, Captain. What kind of noise?"

"I can't figure it out."

"Is it a mechanical sound?"

"No, Sir."

"Electronic?"

"No, Sir."

"Well, what is it?"

"It's ..."

"Yes?"

"It's ..."

"Yes?"

"It's a meow, Sir."

Booker stopped writing. It occurred to him that he had not named his characters. Characters weren't complete without names.

What would be a good name for a cat?

He usually had no trouble thinking of names.

Names could tell a lot about a person. Take Germ. He looked at the stains on the front of Germ's T-shirt and the smudge of chocolate above his eyebrow.

He just *looked* like a germ. That's why no one ever called him Howard.

And Booker. What a great name for someone who loved books. Much better than his real name, Walter.

Some of his best characters had started with a name: Captain Dirtex, Moon Mummy, or his best name yet, Monstroid.

So what should he name his cat? Felina? Leopardo? Lionardo?

Yes, Lionardo. That was it!

He wrote the name in his notebook.

"Booker?"

Booker looked up at the kids filing from the room. Mrs. Brite was standing beside his desk.

"Are you finished with your dialogue?"

He closed his notebook quickly. "Yes."

"I hope you'll be joining us after school for the writing club. I know how much you like to write."

"Thanks," said Booker. "I'll try to come." He gathered his books.

"Mrs. Brite." Germ poked his head back into the room. "Are limericks okay for the writing club?"

"Limericks are perfect." She smiled. Booker was forgotten. "I'm so glad that you'll be joining us, Germ. You have such great potential as a writer."

Limericks! Potential!

Booker stood and walked down the hall with Germ. He couldn't figure out why he was so irritated with his friend.

It was a day like any other. A day of sunshine, laughter, children playing . . . at first. Then slowly a dark shadow moved across the sky. "What is it?" the children cried as they ran to their houses. The wind picked up and the birds called nervously. The shadow began to eclipse the sun.

Eclipso the Evil.

"Hey, I got another one," Germ said. "There once was

a girl named Sue . . . who had an encounter with glue."

"I'm sick of limericks," Booker interrupted. "Limericks are not real writing. Limericks are dumb."

Germ stopped and stared at Booker, his hand grasping his chest. "Wounded," he said dramatically.

Booker was surprised at himself. He had wielded a weapon just like some of the characters in his novels. Only his weapon had been words.

"Thanks a lot," said Germ as he turned away. "Friend!" He turned back and looked at Booker. "You know, your writing is not so great either. Try something besides those dumb science fiction stories sometime."

Booker watched Germ walk away.

Germ had weapons, too.

The war between Earth Boy and Eclipso the Evil had begun. Earth Boy would not be wiped out by the darkness of Eclipso. Somehow he would find a way to defeat his evil foe.

(6)

Meteor Shower

Booker hesitated outside Mrs. Brite's room after school. Should he go in? Should he join the writer's club?

He was a writer, a *published* writer, too, after his speech was printed in the *Pickle Springs Times* last year.

He watched the kids go in one by one. There was Julia Coogan, the girl who always wore black. There was Brad Harper, a guy in his math class. Germ hurried by without looking at him.

The air changed density. Eclipso the Evil had arrived.

Mrs. Brite spotted him. "Come on in, Booker," she called out. Booker walked in behind Germ and settled into a seat. The desks were arranged in a circle.

"Everyone knows everyone else?" Mrs. Brite asked. They all nodded.

"Shall I cut these for you, Mrs. Brite?" Germ was sitting near the brownies.

"Not yet, Germ. We'll have our meeting first."

"I could taste one to make sure they're okay."

"That's all right, Germ. We'll all read our work," said Mrs. Brite. "Then we'll talk about it."

"Then we'll eat?" Germ said.

Mrs. Brite nodded. "If you don't want to read today just say 'pass.' Julia, would you like to start?"

Julia read a long poem about a boy with golden hair. Booker wondered if it was really about Bo Kinney, the star player of the high school football team.

Everyone liked the poem.

Brad read a paragraph about a horse who wanted to go to school.

They talked about the horse and his feelings.

When it was Germ's turn, he stood and read his limerick. Everyone clapped and laughed. Everyone except Booker. Mrs. Brite blushed with pleasure. Germ crossed his eyes at Booker.

"Booker?" Mrs. Brite said. He held his Space Cat story proudly and began to read.

"Meow!

"There was a soft meow from the interior of the space capsule as it sat on the launch ramp."

Germ coughed.

"Meow!

"Louder this time as strange noises came from the control panel."

Germ sneezed.

When he finished there was silence.

Booker looked around the circle. Why wasn't anyone applauding?

"I don't get it," Julia said. "Like how does he breathe and stuff if it was an unmanned spaceship?"

Brad joined in. "How did he get into NASA? I mean would they really let a cat into the space center? I went to space camp last summer and I don't think a cat would be allowed in the control room."

Booker's mouth opened and closed like a fish. What was this? Where was the acclaim? The praise?

As he held his notebook he felt suddenly vulnerable and exposed, like when you were the last one left in a game of dodgeball, or like those dreams where you come to school in your underwear.

As Booker listened to the group dissect his story, it seemed to disintegrate before his eyes.

He remembered something Katherine Paterson had once said, from his book of famous writing quotes: *The two creatures most to be pitied are the spider and the novelist—their lives hanging by a thread spun out of their own guts.*

"Actually," he said finally, "it's fiction."

"Well," said Mrs. Brite, "I love your imagination! We enjoyed that, Booker."

Two more kids read their stories, but Booker didn't listen. They ate the brownies, but Booker hardly tasted them. He was thinking about his story and what people had said. He could not believe that someone could write a story about a horse that went to school but not believe that a cat could be launched into outer space.

"Here's your assignment for next week," Mrs. Brite said when it was time to leave. "Remember last week when we studied point of view in class?" Everyone nodded. "For our next club meeting, try to write a story from an unusual perspective."

Booker was intrigued by the idea. It reminded him of his thoughts about the driving lesson. He might write about that for next time. *If* he came next time.

"Mrs. Brite?"

"Yes, Germ."

"Will there be refreshments next time?"

Mrs. Brite smiled. "Of course," she answered.

Booker gathered his things and walked out into the hall alone. Behind him, Germ paused outside Mrs. Brite's door to tell a group of kids another limerick. This one was about the principal, Mr. Oxford.

"There once was a principal named Ox," Germ said. Immediately there were cheers and whistles.

"Who had a nose like a fox."

More cheers.

Booker frowned and walked faster. He didn't want to hear the rest. As he turned the corner, he ran into Mr. Oxford.

"Hello, Walter," Mr. Oxford said.

"Hello, Mr. Oxford," Booker said. "You might want to

stop by Mrs. Brite's room. I think Germ Germondo wrote a poem about you."

"Oh." Mr. Oxford straightened his tie. He seemed pleased. "I'll go right now and ask him to recite it for me."

Booker felt a strange jolt of energy as he watched Mr. Oxford turn the corner toward Germ. He hurried out the door of the school with a feeling of exhilaration.

Earth Boy launched his first missile, the Oxford Special, toward Eclipso the Evil. Soon defeat would be complete.

Booker held his notebook tighter as he walked home. The criticism of his story still made him wince. All the way home he thought about the writing club. He opened his notebook and reread the first chapter. How *did* the cat breathe? He sat down on the curb and wrote:

Fortunately for the cat, the ship had been equipped for a manned mission. It was a trial run for testing the life systems.

There. He thought about the other comments. Were they right? Should he change everything and start over? He was comforted by the words of Jon Scieszka: *If you want to be a writer, don't listen to any advice given by writers*. He didn't want to think about the writing club. He would write instead.

There was a sharp bump as something hit the side of the ship. Meteors! Another smacked against the ship, hurling Lionardo through the air and crashing him down on the hard metal floor.

The kitten crouched low under the control panel as sharp craggy balls of rock whizzed by on all sides of the ship.

Another hit. Then another. Cruel, uncaring rocks!

As the ship was hit one more time the kitten was thrown against a small lever labeled Warp Speed. Instantly the ship sped out of the flying projectiles.

Lionardo licked his bruises and meowed softly. He had come through the storm alive.

He would survive.

(7)

The Laundry That
Ate Poughkeepsie

As Booker approached the house he saw one of Libba's red athletic socks on the doormat beside her soccer shoes.

He shuddered.

The lone sock reminded him of every horror movie or scary story in existence. They always started with one seemingly harmless detail. One sock or one T-shirt. But soon there would be more, piles and piles of laundry creeping through the house.

The clothes would become threatening and evil as events spun out of control. The laundry would ooze out of the windows, then roll over the neighborhood smothering everything in its path.

He tried out a title in his mind. *The Laundry That Ate Cincinnati.* No. Cincinnati was wrong. He needed a better place.

He dropped his backpack inside the front door and pulled out his notebook, the one where he kept his ideas. He opened it to the section where he recorded great names to use in his books.

There was a page for people, one for dogs, and finally he reached the one for places. He read down the list. Anaheim, Cumberland, Poughkeepsie. "Poughkeepsie!" He said aloud. It was perfect.

The Laundry That Ate Poughkeepsie.

"Booker," Libba called from the laundry room, "are you home?"

"No," he called back.

"Very funny," she said. "Come here."

On the way to the laundry room he encountered a series of dropped garments. He remembered his story and shuddered.

"Is it safe to come in?" he called to Libba from the laundry room door.

"Yes, Dweeb Brain. Mom told me to teach you how to do the laundry."

Booker looked into the laundry room. There were heaps of dirty clothes everywhere. Libba was standing barefoot surrounded by a pile of dirty towels.

The towels moved—just a tremor at first. Then one corner began to twine around the girl's leg.

"Watch," she said. Her ponytail bobbed as she opened the washer. "Here's how you put them in. Wash *like* clothes together. Balance the load. . . ."

Her voice went on and on but Booker's ears had stopped listening.

"This is A-5 unit from the U.S. Army calling B-47. Do you read?"

"We read."

"We have a situation here. Do you read?"

"We read. What's the situation A-5? Enemy invaders? Natural disaster?"

"Negative B-47. It's laundry!"

"When the buzzer goes off, put them in the dryer and start another load." She paused and looked at him. "Have you got that?" she asked.

He nodded.

"Don't forget to wash my underwear," Libba called as she walked out.

"Too bad if I shrink it all," Booker said, listening to the washer fill up with water. How long would it take the load of clothes to finish? He wished that he had paid more attention to Libba. It seemed confusing.

He walked back through the house and went to find Pop. Pop was sitting on the back porch leaning over a box of fishing flies. The sun was beginning to set and the air was cool. Pop didn't notice Booker at first, as he was concentrating on the tiny collection of feathers in front of him under a magnifying glass. He wore his leather slippers, and his sweater was still inside out.

"Ha!" he said to himself, "a Yellow Humpy. Perfection."

Booker smiled. Pop made things seem normal and safe.

Just then, Pop noticed Booker and waved him over. "I made this myself, a while ago." Booker sat down beside Pop, took the fishing fly, and studied it. It was a work of art. It seemed very much like a real bug, but when you looked closer you could see that it was made of feathers and colored thread tied around a tiny gold fishhook.

He settled back comfortably in the porch chair and looked at the box on the table. "What's that one?" Booker pointed to a green fly.

"That one's a Zug Bug." Pop tapped the next compartment. "This one's a Gray Ghost." Pop rubbed his finger over the top of the box.

The backyard was bathed in shade. The trampoline, set off to the side like a big black hole, made him think of his parents. "Have you ever been to Mexico?" he asked Pop.

Pop opened the plastic box with shaky hands and Booker dropped the Yellow Humpy in a compartment.

Pop shook his head. "I've never been anywhere outside Arkansas."

"Me either," said Booker. "Did you ever want to?"

"No. Everything I loved was right here. Daisy, the

river, my writing." He lifted up his glasses and rubbed his eyes.

Booker thought about his grandmother, who had died several years ago. He thought about Pop's house on the river. They had rented it out for a while after Pop had fallen and moved in with them, but now it was empty again. Booker remembered the good times they had there. "Do you miss the river?" he asked.

"Every day," Pop answered.

"I love the river, too," Booker said.

Pop sighed. "I spent my whole life by that river. But now it seems I can only remember parts of it. Glimpses." His voice trailed off.

They sat in silence looking out at the darkening backyard. It was peaceful and quiet.

"Whenever anything went wrong in my life," Pop said into the quiet, "I could always look out at the river and feel better."

He pulled his walker up beside his chair and began to lift himself up. "I'd just look out at that water and know that God made it, that there was something out there bigger than me. Knowing that always made my own problems seem pretty small."

Pop's words settled on Booker with a weight he could not lift. Pop looked at Booker. "I think I'll read a little before dinner," he said.

Pop walked slowly into the house balanced on his silver walker. His arms looked too thin to support him. His feet shuffled forward in the leather slippers.

Booker walked with him and helped him to the bed and put the walker beside the nightstand. Pop lay back with a groan and reached over for his journal. Instead of reading it, he rested it on his chest and closed his eyes.

Booker tiptoed out of the room and hurried to his typewriter. He thought of Lionardo blasting off alone into space, and he wished that it could be him, leaving this house and its sadness. He turned the typewriter on and listened to its whirring.

When he wrote, everything else in his life disappeared and there was only the story. He wanted that now. A way to turn off thoughts of his parents and of Germ and of Pop.

Lionardo sat up and looked around. He had left the meteor shower far behind and now everything was quiet. There was no sound but the hum of the engines. When he looked out the window he could see the beauty of space, endless stars.

There were no problems here, nothing to worry about— only peace and solitude.

"Wash is done!" Libba called out. Booker sighed, the mood broken. There would be no peace or solitude for him.

Booker Jones
Pickle Springs, AR

October 1

Hamerstein Books
New York, NY

Dear Editor,

   Enclosed are two more chapters of my novel <u>Space Cat:
Alone in Space</u>.

   I wanted to run some additional ideas by you for future
books. <u>Brain Mix-up Ray</u>: The brain mix-up ray takes over
the minds of parents. <u>Eclipso the Evil</u>: A boy's best friend
takes over his identity. <u>The Laundry That Ate Poughkeepsie</u>:
Laundry takes over a house. I have always heard, "Write
about what you know." As William Faulkner put it: "Writing
is one third imagination, one third experience, and one third
observation." Unfortunately, I know about these things.

Observing and experiencing too much,
Booker Jones

P.S. I respect your publishing company as I have discovered
you have not published one single limerick. This is a sign of
quality.

(8)

Iridescent Ooooze

Booker and Libba sat down at the table to eat. Pop was lying on his bed with his journal still on his chest. They had decided to let him sleep.

On the table was a rectangular glass baking dish filled with a gray mixture. There was a hole in the center where Libba had probably stuck her finger to test the temperature. At any temperature it would be grim.

"Eat," Sistoid said. "Eat the foul food of my people." The boy backed away. "No!" he said. "I'll never eat it. Noo! I'd rather . . ."

Plop!

He blinked as the mixture was plopped onto his plate. "Tuna Surprise," Libba said.

Surprise seemed like an odd word to name a food. He remembered the definition from his vocabulary test last year: *A sudden unexpected attack or assault.*

On second thought, it was perfectly named.

"I learned to make it in Life Skills class."

"Did you pass?" Booker asked.

Libba's eyes narrowed. "What kind of question is that?"

"Look for yourself."

Booker pointed to the pile of Tuna Surprise on his plate. Liquid oozed out from the sides of the gray mixture. Was he mistaken, or did it glow?

They glared at each other for a moment across the table.

"Try it," she said. "It's not like Mom's here to cook us anything."

Slowly he lifted the fork to his mouth with one hand. He held his nose with the other. He closed his eyes and swallowed the casserole. Fish and chemicals.

Libba smiled. "I knew you'd like it," she said as she picked up her own fork. "Don't forget what Mom always says: 'Clean your plate.'"

He steeled himself to finish the dinner.

"I made dessert, too," Libba said. She pointed to the oven, where small wisps of smoke were emerging.

"I'm full," Booker said as Libba raced to the oven to remove a black lump in a cake pan. He took advantage of her distraction to scrape his plate into the garbage.

He stopped by the laundry room and put the wet clothes into the dryer. He still needed to put one more load of clothes in the washer. He was confused. What had Libba said? *Like* clothes together. What exactly did that mean? *Like* meant things that were the same. He dumped in all Libba's underwear, then her socks. Last, he put in the red athletic socks and closed the lid. Done.

Booker hurried back to his typewriter. The dinner had inspired him. His mind was filled with an image of oozing iridescent liquid. Time for one more chapter before bed.

He began to type.

The meteors had damaged the ship. Now as it zoomed through darkest space, a drop of iridescent liquid began to ooze from a new crack in the radiation containment system.

"Me-ow!" Lionardo was thirsty. He eyed the drop with suspicion. It glowed.

"Me-ow?" Another drop oozed out.

The nuclear fuel was leaking. It was radioactive, with the power to alter genetic material.

"Me-ow." Lionardo moved toward the liquid.

He touched a drop with his paw. It was warm. He was confused by the glow, but he was very thirsty.

He lapped the drop up. It tasted like fish and chemicals.

Me-OW!!!

He drank another drop. Me-OW OW!!!

As he drank, an amazing transformation began to take place:

His tiny body grew at a tremendous rate until soon he was as big as a man.

His face looked wiser, more intelligent, less catlike.

Lionardo changed from a mere kitten to a super-powered cat. He was . . . Space Cat!

Booker sighed contentedly as he pulled the page out of the typewriter. He looked at the clock beside him. It was his usual bedtime, but who cared. There was no one to tell him to go to bed anyway.

As he walked to the bathroom to brush his teeth, he stopped by Pop's room. Pop was still lying on his bed with his journal on his chest, but his eyes were open.

"Hi, Pop, you want some dinner?"

Pop shook his head.

"Just as well," Booker said. "Libba cooked."

The corners of Pop's mouth turned up in a slight smile.

"Bad?" he asked.

"Bad," Booker answered. "I could make you a sandwich."

"No thanks," Pop answered. "I'll see you in the morning."

Booker stood in the hall for a moment. He could hear Libba talking on the phone in her room. No one said, "Get to bed," or "Is your homework done?" It was odd. He missed his parents in a way but it was also a different feeling to be able to choose for himself what to do. He went to his room and kicked his backpack into the corner. No homework tonight he decided. Instead he would write.

"Me-ow," Lionardo said as he stretched his new muscles. "Let's see what this ship can do." He was speaking!

Ground control heard the voice on their radio and called in.

"Who's up there!?"

Lionardo pushed the throttle forward and took control of the ship.

"Surprise!" he answered as he blasted even further into outer space.

(9)

My Ex-Best Friend

Sistoid had taken the city captive. She holed herself up in the most desirable fortress and greedily dominated it.

Booker waited for Libba to finish in the bathroom. It was almost time for the school bus. He knocked again.

"Booker! Go away! You know Mom said I could have fifteen minutes every morning in the bathroom."

Booker stepped back and leaned against the wall to wait for his turn. He only had a few minutes before the bus would come.

"It's been twenty minutes," he said. "Twenty-one."

"It's going to take even longer if you keep disturbing me."

Booker stopped by Pop's door and looked in at his grandfather who was still in bed. The silver walker rested beside the bed.

"Pop?"

Pop opened his eyes.

"You want some breakfast?"

"No thanks, Booker."

"Are you okay?"

"I'm just tired," Pop said. "I'll eat later."

Booker heard the bathroom door open and close but before he could even move Libba called, "Bus!"

"I gotta go." Booker stood to leave.

"Where's your mother?" Pop asked.

Booker looked at Pop closely. Was it a joke? When he looked at Pop's face he saw sincerity.

"She's in Mexico, Pop," Booker said. "Don't you remember?"

"Bus!" Libba called again. Booker hesitated. "Are you okay?" he said.

Pop closed his eyes. "Yes," he said.

"Are you sure you'll be okay?"

Pop nodded.

"Come on, Dweeb Brain," Libba said. "It's here!"

"Pop, I'll see you as soon as I get home."

Pop didn't answer.

"Come on!" Libba grabbed his arm and pulled him out. "If we miss the bus we have to walk."

They ran to the bus. The seat that Germ usually saved for him was taken—by Brad Harper from the writing club. Booker didn't want to sit by Germ anyway. As he walked by he was careful not to look at him.

Booker had an uneasy feeling about leaving Pop. It

would have been nice to talk to Germ about it. Germ always made everything seem better.

Every time he glanced up he saw Germ looking at him. Germ looked away quickly. Booker opened his notebook to take his mind off of Germ.

Lionardo stretched his new muscles. He pointed and flexed his new razor-sharp claws. He blinked his X-ray vision eyes twice and looked around the spaceship.

Lionardo didn't need anything. He didn't need anyone. He could make it just fine.

The thrusters sputtered once as the ship moved forward. The engines sounded a little funny but everything was still working.

Booker looked up at Germ. Germ was writing in his notebook, too. He could see Germ lift up his notebook to show Brad what he had written. Brad laughed. The very sight of Germ writing made Booker angry. He renewed his efforts.

Lionardo picked up the microphone. Instead of meowing he said in a clear voice. "Mission Control, this is Lionardo. I am taking control of the ship."

"Lionardo?" the crackling voice of mission control came over the speaker. "Who are you? This is supposed to be an unmanned spaceship!"

"Ha!" Lionardo laughed. "You are correct, it is unmanned."

"Then who are you? What are you?"

Lionardo grinned catlike and answered clearly into the microphone. "The spaceship is unmanned but it's not <u>uncatted</u>."

"Hey, we're here." The voice of the bus driver penetrated his thoughts.

"Sorry," Booker said. He gathered his things and walked up the aisle. On Germ's seat was a folded piece of paper. On the front it read, "Booker." He picked it up as he went by.

Outside, he opened it and read.

> *A boy's best friend was a traitor*
> *as mean as a snake or a gator.*
> *The principal heard*
> *a discouraging word*
> *And the boy got detention hall later.*
>
> *Thanks a lot!*
>
> *Signed: Your Ex-best Friend*

Germ was still mad.

(10)

Places

"Today we will focus on setting," Mrs. Brite said as creative writing class began.

Booker opened his notebook in anticipation.

"Everyone think about a place. Close your eyes and visualize that place. What does it look like? What would you hear? What does it smell like? What would you taste there? What would you feel?"

Booker closed his eyes. He tried to think of a place but he couldn't. His family was in so many places. His parents were in Mexico. Libba was at school like he was. And Pop was at home. For some reason, the thought of Pop, home alone, made his stomach tighten.

"Booker do you have a problem?"

Booker opened his eyes. All around him kids were writing.

"No, Mrs. Brite, I'm just thinking." He looked at his paper and tried to concentrate.

He turned the page and thought about Lionardo. Where was he headed? A new destination. Who did he miss? No one. How would he survive alone? Easily.

He tried to think of the assignment. What did Lionardo see?

Lionardo looked out the window of the spaceship. The setting around him was beautiful. He could see a million gleaming stars, a bright purple supernova in the distance. A shooting star shot past the window in a burst of golden sparks.

What did he hear?

He heard the rumble of the thrusters and the occasional beeps from the ship's computer.

What did he smell?

He could still smell the iridescent radioactive fuel. It smelled delicious.

Taste?

Fish and chemicals.

What did he feel?

He felt the movement of the ship as it traveled onward. The metal control stick was cold in his hands as he pushed it forward.

All was peaceful.

"Mrs. Brite?"

"Yes, Germ?"

"I'm done. You want to hear mine?"

"Of course."

"Is it all right if I made it in the form of a limerick?"
She nodded.

> *"The school cafeteria smells crude.*
> *The sounds of the children are rude.*
> *But you can survive*
> *And even stay alive*
> *As long as you don't eat the food."*

The class burst into laughter and applause. Booker
did not join in.

"Why, Howard," Mrs. Brite said. "That is very funny.
Let's see if we can publish it in the school paper."

Lionardo pushed the thruster control forward. It was
time to move on. Anyplace would be better than this.

Hamerstein Books
New York, NY

September 27

Booker Jones
Pickle Springs, AR

Dear Mr. Jones,

We regret that your novel MONSTROID does not meet the needs of our list. Good luck placing it elsewhere.

Sincerely,

Hamerstein Books

Hamerstein Books
New York, NY

September 28

Booker Jones
Pickle Springs, AR

Dear Mr. Jones,

We regret that your novel MONSTROID II does not meet the needs of our list. Good luck placing it elsewhere.

Sincerely,

Hamerstein Books

(11)

On Strike

The piles of clothing grew at an incredible rate of speed. No
sooner was one load terminated than another would spring
to life. As the boy innocently walked by the laundry room a
shirtsleeve reached up and grabbed him. It pulled him deep
into the suffocating pile. Deeper. Deeper.

"Help," he called out. "Help!"

No one answered.

Booker loaded one more pile of towels into the wash-
ing machine. Where were all these clothes coming from?
It was endless. He put in as many towels as he could,
then looked around the room for the detergent.

He was tired of laundry. He heard Libba coming
down the hall and hoped she would give him a hand.

Libba burst into the room red-faced. "All my underwear is pink!" Libba held up a handful of pink under-
pants. "What did you do to them?" She stood in the
laundry room with an expression of horror on her face.

"I don't know what I did," Booker said, shrugging. "I'm trying."

"You didn't wash my red socks with my white things, did you?"

"You said wash *like* things together," Booker said.

"Dweeb Brain! That means *colors* that are alike. You don't wash red things with white things."

She threw a pair of pink underwear at him.

Booker lifted his hands to protect himself. She threw another. Then another. He was showered with pink clothes.

"You are such a dork!"

Libba left. Booker looked at the pile of pink underwear. This was all too confusing. Libba returned with an armload of things for him to wash. "Now wash this one for tomorrow," she said with a scowl, "and have my soccer uniform ready for Thursday and *don't* ruin anything this time!"

Booker closed the washer. The lid banged shut.

"Do it yourself," he said, and he walked back toward his room.

"It's your job." Libba followed him still carrying the clothes. "Mom said you have to do it."

"Go tell Mom then," Booker said. "I'm on strike."

Libba stopped dead still in the hall and stared at him. "Strike?" she said in disbelief. "You are on strike? Then I'm on strike, too. No dinner!"

"Good," Booker said. "No dinner is an improvement!"

Booker walked back to his room and slammed the door. He heard Libba's bedroom door slam. The week had gone from bad to worse.

His rejection letters were on his desk, reminding him of his failure. He stared at the letters for a few moments then decided to talk to Pop about them.

"Pop?" Booker went into Pop's room and turned on the light. Pop was still lying on the bed.

"Yes?" he answered, blinking in the sudden brightness.

"I'm rejected."

"Let's see." Pop pulled himself up into a sitting position and grappled on the nightstand for his glasses. He took the letters from Booker and read them. Then he sighed. "He could have at least signed his name," Pop said.

Booker sat down on the foot of the bed cross-legged.

"I thought this might be the one," said Booker. "*Monstroid* was one of my favorite books to write. Now all that work is wasted."

"Writing is never wasted," Pop said, handing the letters back. "You learned something from writing that."

Booker took the letters.

"Even writing that's not published is still writing. Like this book." Pop patted the journal. "It helps me relive things. Brings back my memories."

Pop picked up the journal and opened it.

"Listen to this," he said. He began to read:

"I heard her again last night. Daisy tried to be quiet and let me sleep. But I heard her slipping out of the bedroom at about three o'clock this morning. So I got up, too, and I made her a cup of tea and I made myself one and we sat together in the darkness out on the porch listening to the river, sipping our tea."

There was silence for a moment. Then Booker spoke.

"Why don't you write anymore, Pop?"

Pop shook his head. "I think my stories are all done," he said. "I'm reading to see what I did."

Booker leaned back against the wall.

"I'm trying to remember," Pop said.

"What?"

"The river. I can't see it anymore. I can't quite get my mind around it. Green. That's all I can see. I used to be able to recall it when I looked at things that reminded me of the river—like my fishing flies. And it used to help to read about the river in my journal. But it's so fuzzy now. Just green."

Pop was staring at Booker. Booker felt like he needed to do something for Pop but he didn't know what to do.

"Can I make you a cup of tea?"

Pop lay back. "No," he said. "But thanks." Pop's journal was open on his lap.

Pop closed his eyes. Booker sat quietly on the bed and looked at his grandfather. *Think detail* he told himself. Pop had worn the same clothes ever since his parents left. Pop's thin shoulders poked out underneath the gray sweater. He was thinner than Booker had remembered. And his hands . . . Booker looked at the hand lying across the journal. It trembled a little.

Booker looked at the door. There seemed to be no escape from the unhappiness of his situation. He had come here for comfort but it seemed now that he needed to comfort Pop. Unfortunately he didn't know how to do that any more than he knew how to wash the clothes.

Booker walked slowly back to his room. He couldn't do anything now but write.

A call came over the speaker.

Lionardo listened closer. The voice was different from any he had ever heard before. It wasn't human, like mission control—it was catlike!

The voice spoke again. He couldn't understand the language, but it seemed to be calling for help.

Lionardo froze, his hand on the microphone button.

He listened to the call for help one more time then switched off the radio. What could he do anyway?

It was all too disturbing. He had enough trouble just worrying about himself.

Booker Jones
Pickle Springs, AR

October 3

Hamerstein Books
New York, NY

Dear Fiend,

I'm sorry that my novel <u>Monstroid</u> does not meet the needs of your list. I'm sorry <u>Monstroid II</u> also does not meet the needs of your list.

Many of the great books of all times were rejected at first. <u>A Wrinkle in Time</u> was rejected for over two years. Dr. Seuss's first book, 43 times.

When George Orwell's book <u>Animal Farm</u> was sent to a publisher they wrote back and said, "It is impossible to sell animal stories in the U.S.A." <u>Animal Farm</u> went on to sell millions.

I'm in great company.

Crushed but not defeated,
Booker Jones

Booker Jones
Pickle Springs, AR

October 4

Hamerstein Books
New York, NY

Dear Friend,

Sorry! When I wrote to you about my <u>Monstroid</u> books I wrote to you as fiend instead of friend. It was a MISTAKE! Amazing the difference one letter can make in a word. A fiend in my pocket dictionary is: a diabolically cruel or wicked person. A friend is: a person who is on good terms with another; one who is not hostile.

I am sure you are not a FIEND!

Let's not let one little r come between us and a new career.

On good terms and not hostile,
Booker Jones

(12)

Felini

"Did anyone complete the assignment?" Mrs. Brite looked hopefully at the writing club. "You've had a whole week."

Booker thought back over the week. All was chaos.

His parents would not be home for four more days and the house was looking grim.

Mail and newspapers were piled high in the hall. Pizza boxes covered the kitchen table. Dirty clothes were everywhere. Booker smoothed his wrinkled T-shirt. It was the same one that he had worn yesterday. He had even slept in it.

Now that no one was making him do anything, he had stopped doing everything. Laundry, homework—he had even stopped brushing his teeth.

Pop was not doing much either. He only wanted to read out of his journal, and the entries he chose to read were becoming sadder and sadder. It made Booker sad to listen to them.

Booker looked around the circle where all the kids were getting out their notebooks. He hadn't wanted to come to the writing club but anything was better than going home.

"Who would like to begin?" Mrs. Brite asked the group. "Remember, the exercise was to write from an unusual point of view. Did anyone try it?"

Booker looked down at his notebook. He had chosen the latest chapter of his book to read, but now he was sorry. The memory of the last time he had read his Space Cat story for the writing club wasn't a happy one.

"What kind of cookies are those?" Germ asked. Germ had on a clean shirt today, and his hair was combed. He looked less germ-like, more Howard-like.

"We'll have the cookies later, Howard." Mrs. Brite smiled at Germ.

"I just wondered."

"Chocolate chip."

"With nuts?"

"Yes, Howard. Now, why don't you go first?"

"I just did one point of view," said Germ. "My dad's."

"That's fine," Mrs. Brite said.

"It's in the form of a limerick," said Germ.

Booker slouched lower in his seat. More limericks.

Germ opened his notebook. "My Dad." He looked around the room. "Ready?"

Mrs. Brite nodded.

"I lived a wonderful life
without a single strife.
Two kids and a dog,
a cat and a frog,
and a wonderful cook for a wife."

Everyone applauded politely. "My dad doesn't really have a frog," Germ said. "That's just the only word that would rhyme."

"Let's brainstorm," Mrs. Brite said. She looked around the circle. "What other word could Germ use?"

The kids began to call out words. "Log." "Bog." "Tog." "Fog."

"Maybe something with cat and fat instead," said Julia. "That might go with the wonderful cook part. Is your dad fat?"

"Wait . . . wait. . . ." Germ said excitedly.

He put his hand dramatically to his head.

"Quiet . . . quiet," he said. Then, "Aha! I've got it.

"My Dad." He paused. "Ready?"

Mrs. Brite nodded.

"I lived a wonderful life
without a single strife.
Two kids and cat,
but a little bit fat,
with a wonderful cook for a wife."

"Bravo!" said Mrs. Brite. She clapped her hands together.

"Good work, group. Who's next?"

"I did an imaginary interview with a horse," Brad said. "It's a horse's point of view of the Kentucky Derby."

"Wonderful!" Mrs. Brite responded. "Will you read it for us?"

Brad cleared his throat and began: "Neigh! said the horse."

Booker stopped listening. He was still thinking about home and Pop. Stacks of mail and pizza boxes.

"Booker?"

Booker sat up with a start at the sound of his name.

"Yes?"

Everyone was staring at him.

"Will you read for us?"

"Mine's a little different," he said. The notebook in his hand trembled. "It's another chapter from my newest book, *Space Cat: Alone in Space*. It's the point of view of two different cats. I call it, 'A Tale of Two Kitties.'"

Germ snickered.

Mrs. Brite looked hard at Germ.

"Go ahead," she said to Booker.

Booker read.

Lionardo: Lionardo stared at the radio. It was still turned off. He didn't want to hear the strange voice calling for help. To avoid it he had traveled through the Milky Way and across the galaxies—far, far away from the pleading voice.

Felini: "Hello, . . . Hello. . . . Is anyone out there . . . ? Hello. Does anyone hear me? I'm calling from the Dog Star. Is there someone out there who can understand me? I need help. Fast. I can't last much longer. Will anyone come to my rescue? Anyone. . . . Anyone. . . ."

Lionardo: It was peaceful in the spaceship. Lionardo only had to worry about himself. "ME-ow," he said. "ME-ow! There is only ME."

Felini: "Hello? Can anyone help? Does anyone hear? I'm getting weaker . . . weaker . . ."

Lionardo: "Me-ow! ME! ME! ME!"

Felini: Anyone . . . Anyone . . . Any—"

There was not a sound when Booker finished reading.

"Why doesn't Lionardo help him?" Julia said.

"Because he doesn't hear him," Brad said. "He won't turn on the radio."

"Why won't he answer the radio?" asked Julia. She sounded distressed. "Felini might die."

They all looked at Booker, waiting for answers.

He couldn't answer. His throat had tightened up.

"Booker?" Mrs. Brite said.

Booker put his head in his hands. When Julia said Felini might die, the words burned in his brain and hurt him. But it wasn't Felini he was worried about—it was Pop. Pop was slipping away from them. First not eating.

Then not remembering. He was retreating from life. Was there a cry for help that Booker was missing? Was it already too late?

"I've got to go home," he said to Mrs. Brite. "I've got to do something."

"You can't stay for cookies?"

Booker didn't answer. He was already headed out the door.

(13)

Motionless

Booker hurried down the hall to the office. He could use the phone to call Pop. His brain raced ahead of him with frightful images: Pop on the floor, fallen beside his walker; Pop in bed too weak to get up. A good imagination was vital to a writer but dangerous when you were worried. He stopped imagining.

"Can I use the phone?" he asked the secretary.

"*May* I use the phone," she said. She pointed to the phone on the extra desk.

Booker picked up the receiver and dialed nervously, his finger pressing too hard on the buttons.

It rang. It rang again. It rang a third time. He held his breath. No answer. Booker put the phone receiver back.

A new finger of fear poked at him. He had to get home, but he was afraid to go alone. He thought of Libba and ran down to the soccer field where she was practicing.

He waved her over.

"I just called home," he said, "and Pop didn't answer the phone."

"He's probably asleep, Dweeb Brain," she said. But her eyes had a nervous look.

She looked at her watch. "Let's go home," she said.

They started walking slowly toward the house, but the closer they got the faster they walked. By the time they turned the corner to their own street they were both running. They ran into the house to Pop's door. It was closed.

They stood in front of the closed door breathing hard. Booker tapped on the door.

No answer.

"Open it," Libba said.

Staring at the closed door, Booker was suddenly afraid. What if something had happened to Pop?

"You open it," Booker said. "You're older."

"Let's do it together."

They put their hands on the doorknob and slowly opened the door. The room was dim. They could see Pop on the bed, motionless.

"Pop?" Libba said.

He didn't move.

"Pop?" Libba said again, and her voice trembled. "Oh, no." She grabbed Booker's arm so tightly that the blood stopped flowing.

"Huh?" Pop jerked suddenly and opened his eyes.

Booker and Libba both let out sighs of relief.

"You scared us," Libba said. She sat down on the bed beside Pop and took his hand. Booker sat on the chair beside the bed. He was still out of breath from the run home. But each breath he blew out seemed to be relief.

Pop blinked. "I scared you?"

"We called and you didn't answer."

"We were worried," Booker added.

"I'm fine," Pop said. "Is it morning?"

Booker looked at Libba. "No," he said. "We just got home from school."

"I was just resting," Pop said. "Just resting."

"Come out and sit with us," Libba said. "I'll make you something to eat."

Pop didn't move.

"I'll listen, Pop, if you want to read more of your journal to me," Booker said.

Pop shook his head.

"Can we get you anything?"

"No."

Libba looked at Booker and jerked her head toward the door. Together they left the room.

"Is he okay?" Booker whispered to Libba in the hall.

"I don't know," Libba said. "He's acting so strange." They moved into the kitchen and sat down at the kitchen table. The table was littered with dirty cups and pizza boxes. "Everything is out of control," Libba said. "And I don't know what to do."

Booker lifted his hands palm-up in a gesture of help-lessness.

"Let's call Mom and Dad," Libba said. They found the number of the hotel. Libba dialed while Booker sat nervously beside the phone. "It's just ringing and ringing," Libba said. "It must be a wrong number or something."

"Try again," Booker suggested.

"Later," she said. She didn't move. She just sat and stared at the phone.

Booker could not bear to wait. He stood up and paced back and forth in the kitchen a few times wondering whether to go to Pop, or to his room, or to stand beside the phone. He did the only thing he could think of to do. He went to his typewriter and soon he was lost in his words.

Space Cat stared at the microphone. Should he turn it on? He was torn with indecision.

He pushed the button.

"Anyone?" the purry voice said. "Is anyone there?"

This time he could understand! The voice spoke his language!

"This is Felini. I'm being held prisoner by the evil King Canina. Anyone?"

Lionardo could no longer ignore the pleas for help.

"This is Lionardo," he said into the microphone. "Space Cat."

"Please come and rescue me."

Lionardo felt helpless. How could he respond? He didn't know how to work the weapon systems. He didn't know how to find Felini.

He tried Mission Control.

No answer.

He was on his own.

(14)

Crisis

"Booker?" Libba knocked at his door.

"Come in."

Libba came in and sat beside him on the bed. "I tried the hotel again and I still can't get through. I don't know what's wrong with Pop but I'm really worried."

"What can we do?" Booker said.

"Try talking to him again, Booker."

"Me?"

"Yes, he likes to talk to you. I'll come with you."

Booker and Libba went to Pop's room and sat down beside the bed.

"Pop," Booker said. "We're worried about you. You aren't eating and you're in your room in bed all the time. What can we do to help?"

"I can't remember it," he said.

"What?" Booker said.

"I can't remember what my house looks like. What

the river looks like." Booker and Libba looked at each other.

"We can go when Mom and Dad get back," Libba offered.

Pop didn't move. His hands shook a little and a tear squeezed out of the side of his eye. Booker had never seen Pop cry before.

"Pop," he said. "Don't do that." He tucked a tissue under Pop's hands but the hands still didn't move.

Another tear rolled down his cheek.

"Pop, please," Booker said. "Please don't cry."

From beside him he heard a sniffle.

"Libba?" he said. He saw her face screwed up ready to cry, too.

"I don't know what to do," she said. She let out a breath of air and tears came. "This is all too much. Mom and Dad left us because they thought we were responsible enough to handle things. But I can't cook. Everything I make is terrible. Then Pop stopped eating." The last word trailed off in a sob.

Booker looked at Libba and was surprised. He hadn't even thought of things from her point of view.

"It's my fault," he said. "I should have spent more time with Pop."

Booker looked back and forth from Libba to Pop. Pop was so frail. Libba was a mess. It was a crisis.

Part of him wanted to run out the door and speed away like Space Cat—leaving all of this behind. But part of him was crying inside, too. He needed to help Pop.

He thought about Pop's journal and about the river, and he understood that all the things that Pop had been telling him about the river were really cries for help. That somehow, some way, Pop needed to see the river to know that he wasn't alone.

"I have an idea," Booker said.

Pop didn't look up.

"We could go there."

Pop's eyes opened.

Booker licked his lips, then continued. "I know you can't drive anymore," he said to Pop. "But you're a responsible adult, right?" Pop didn't answer.

Libba looked up and smiled through her tears. "I can only drive with a responsible adult."

Booker's voice sped up. "Mom and Dad left the car in the garage. . . ."

"I'll show you the way," Pop said. His voice sounded stronger.

Libba blew her nose. "You'll take the blame with me?" she asked Booker.

"I will," he said. "I promise."

Libba looked at Pop. "We can't go unless you eat," she said.

Pop smiled. "Will you cook me something?" he asked.

Libba tossed her tissue into the trash can and stood up. "I'll make you whatever you want," she said.

Lionardo got up from the chair. He would not let Felini down—he would take control. He had choices. He could choose to sit alone or he could go and rescue Felini. He pointed his ship toward the Dog Star. Into the speaker he gave a battle cry.

"I'm coming Felini. Me-ow!"

(15)

Sistoid Rides Again

When Booker got up the next morning he found Pop sitting on the front porch ready to go. His silver walker was propped up beside him.

The school bus stopped and Pop stood up on shaky legs and waved it on.

"Libba," Booker called out. "Are you coming?"

Libba came out dressed and ready to go. "We're really going to do this?" she asked.

Booker nodded.

"Okay," Libba said. Then she smiled and her eyes twinkled with excitement. "I'll get the car."

Libba walked out to the garage. Booker sat with Pop and waited. They heard the car start up. They heard a screech as the car pulled out of the garage and a bang as it hit the garbage can. Booker looked at Pop. "You're sure you want to do this?"

Pop nodded. His eyes were bright, too.

They bundled Pop into the front seat of the car and helped him buckle his seat belt. Booker got into the back and they began. Libba pulled out of the driveway, inching along in slow motion. At the same time she barely missed the Harbey's mailbox next door.

"Careful," said Pop. "I want to make it there alive."

"Do we have an airbag?" Booker asked.

"Hush," said Libba in a serious voice. "I'm concentrating."

Booker was quiet. He wanted Libba to concentrate. The more she concentrated, the safer they would be.

At the stop sign, Libba put on the brakes too hard. Booker's head whipped back.

"Whoa," Pop said. "Let's take it easy."

Booker expected someone to stop them—a neighbor running out of a house waving and screaming, a cop with flashing lights—but nothing happened. They glided easily out of the neighborhood.

"I've never been on the interstate," Libba said.

"Nothing to it," Pop said. "There's the on ramp. Right there. No, right *there!*"

Libba swung the car onto the on ramp and soon they were driving down the highway.

Creeping was more like it. Cars whizzed past them like they were not even moving.

A truck pulled up close behind them, flashed his lights, then honked.

Libba's hands tightened on the steering wheel.

"You can speed up a little," Pop suggested. The car moved a little faster.

"There's a cop coming," Booker said. He saw the white car coming up behind them. Libba gasped.

"Easy," Pop said.

The cop pulled up beside them and drove along for what seemed like an eternity. Finally he sped off with his siren blaring and lights flashing.

Libba blew out a breath of relief.

"Wow," Booker said. He rested his head back on the seat. His books paled in comparison to driving with Libba.

The characters in his book were always running *away* from something—meteors, asteroids, giant frogs. He had never known it could be just as exciting to run *to* something.

As they rode along Pop dozed and Booker wrote.

He wrote a wonderful rescue scene as Lionardo saved Felini from King Canina and the Dog People and a powerful battle scene as they escaped from the planet.

After an hour had passed Pop woke up. "Here comes the exit," Pop said. "Stay in the left lane. Right here. Now easy does it."

Booker relaxed a little as they pulled off the interstate. Libba was doing great. The roads got smaller and smaller as they neared the river. The traffic lighter and lighter.

Pop slept again as they drove along.

Finally they pulled up into the gravel driveway, the weeds and uncut grass brushing against the car as Libba negotiated the narrow trail. The car bumped over the rough ground.

"Pop, we're here." They stopped.

Pop blinked. "Where?" he asked. He looked around confused.

Then his face beamed as he realized where he was. He grabbed anxiously at the door handle.

"Wait, Pop." Libba put the car in park and turned off the motor. They sat in silence for a moment staring out at the river.

"We made it," Libba said. Pop didn't move. "You all right?" she asked.

Pop nodded.

He was staring at the old house. The yard was overgrown with weeds, and a wisteria vine had grown around the porch and bloomed with bright lavender blossoms. The paint peeled off in long strips.

His gaze turned to the river.

"It's beautiful," Pop said. "I remember."

They looked out at the river. "Look over there," Pop said. "There's where your grandmother and I sat and listened to the bobwhite's call."

"Yeah, Pop," Booker said.

"And there! That old tree was hit by lightning the year we moved in. Scared Daisy near to death." Pop was more and more excited as he pointed out the window. "Booker, do you remember that rock? That's where you caught your first fish."

Booker thought back to Pop's words: "Whenever anything went wrong in my life I could always look out at the river and feel better."

In the rearview mirror his eyes met Libba's and they smiled at each other.

(16)

Rainbow

Libba and Booker opened the car door and helped Pop out. They guided him to an old lounge chair beside the water and Booker ran back to the house for blankets. He tucked one around Pop as Pop settled into the seat with a groan.

Booker spread another blanket on the ground for himself and Libba.

The three of them did not move. They sat watching the river as it moved over rocks and bubbled around boulders. The light filtered down through the trees, reflecting patterns on the water. The sound of the water gurgled around them. Coolness filled the air. A silver trout leapt from the river as if it was putting on a show just for them.

"Rainbow," Pop said. "Rainbow trout."

Booker remembered the other definition of surprise that he had learned: *To strike with wonder.*

It seemed to fit the moment.

Pop took a deep breath like he was trying to breathe it all in. "How could I possibly have forgotten this?" he said. He closed his eyes and leaned back in the lounge chair. "Thank you," he said weakly. "Thank you."

Libba lay back on the blanket and closed her eyes, too, but Booker was mesmerized by the river. As he listened to the water, words flickered in his mind—not like the lightning bolts of his usual ideas but a quiet voice, something softer. The trout and the sun and the beauty of this place moved him and he took out his notebook.

He wrote down what he saw:

Green pines line the banks. Rocks jut out from the river bottom making currents around a tear-shaped sandbar.

He wrote what he heard:

Birds call from the trees and there is the snap of a branch as a deer wanders nearby. The water gurgles as it flows.

He wrote what he could feel here.

Soft moss underneath me. Rough bark on the tree trunks. Cold damp rocks. Icy water.

What could he smell?

Sweet honeysuckle flowers

What could he taste?

A cool drink of river water.

He used the phrases to make a poem and wrote the words in his notebook.

> River.
> Green pines line the banks.
> Rocks jut out making currents
> Around a tear-shaped sandbar.
> Birds call from the trees.
> A branch cracks as a deer wanders nearby.
> The water gurgles as it flows.
> Soft moss. Rough bark. Cold damp rocks. Icy water.
> Sweet honeysuckle flowers. A cool drink.
> River.

Booker pressed the notebook to his chest, filled with the beauty of the place.

He understood writing in a way that he never had before. It wasn't about being in a club or having people admire you, or even about getting published. It was about this—a way to hold on to something beautiful.

He knew this poem was not one he would share. Instead, he'd keep it as a tender memory of his own. He had read in his writer's quote book that there was not a first book or second book, there was only one big book in a writer's life—all the books of a lifetime adding up to one. In the middle of all his science fiction stories this poem would rest, like the purple violet pressed between the pages of Pop's journal.

(17)

Happy Endings

"Drive through McDonald's," said Pop from the passenger seat as they neared the interstate to go home. "I'm starving!"

"Oh, Pop," Libba said. "You feel better!" She looked at him from behind the steering wheel.

In the back seat Booker smiled. He felt a bubbling up of joy that surprised him. They had done it.

Together they had helped Pop. When he looked at Libba she looked different to him—older. He felt proud of her.

Libba swung the car into McDonald's and pulled into the drive-through.

"You want anything?" she asked Booker.

"No, thanks."

She got Pop's food and pulled back out into traffic.

"Good driving," Pop said. "Let's go home." Libba pulled onto the interstate and skillfully moved into traffic.

"Pop?" Booker asked from the back seat.

"Yes?" Pop munched on a french fry.

"Why do you think Mom and Dad went to Mexico?"

"They're just writing another chapter."

"What do you mean?"

Pop thought for a minute.

"Relationships are like books. There's a lot of excitement at the beginning, and joy at watching something new unfold."

Booker watched the forest and trees whiz by and nodded, thinking about his own novels. "The beginning is always easy," he said.

Pop looked back and smiled. "Then you hit the middle and the hard work really begins. But the book must go on even if it's word by torturous word. Finally, after all the hard work, you write a happy ending and your book is complete and whole."

"Like you and Grandma."

Pop nodded. "You have to remember to always add some happy parts."

"Like cups of tea?"

Pop smiled. "Like cups of tea and trips to Mexico."

Libba pulled off of the interstate and slowed down as she drove through the neighborhood.

Booker smiled now when he thought back to his parents dancing to *La cucaracha*. They were just making choices like he did every time he sat down to write a book. He hadn't thought about making choices for himself.

Maybe it was time to write some happier parts in his own life.

Booker thought about the stories he was writing now and in his mind he gave them happy endings.

Sistoid turned her vehicle of destruction into a vehicle of mercy, bringing joy and peace to everyone.

The couple stood looking at the Mexican sunset together. "Thank goodness for the brain mix-up ray," the man said.

The boy and girl watched the giant pile of laundry moving toward them. It was dirty. It was smelly. But together they could beat it.

What about Eclipso the Evil? He thought of his friendship with Germ. Was it like a book? Could he change the ending?

"You know what I want to do?" Pop asked between bites of french fries.

"What, Pop?" Booker said.

"I want to stop by Office Depot and get a new journal. Today is a day we need to remember."

"I'll take you, Pop," Libba said. Booker smiled.

"You know what I want to do?" Libba asked. "Now don't laugh."

"I won't," Booker said and for once he meant it.

"I want to clean up the house for Mom and Dad."

"Clean?"

She nodded. "I just want them to come home and find everything good."

Booker understood. There was something he wanted to make right, too. "I'll help you," he said. "But there's something I have to do first. Will you drop me at Germ's?" he asked.

They drove slowly down the street and stopped at Germ's house. Booker looked out the window.

He thought of all the times he had spent at Germ's house. He remembered when Pop had first moved in with them. Booker had slept at Germ's house every weekend for three months, since he didn't have a real place to sleep at home.

He thought of the fun they had had on Germ's porch playing Monopoly and reading stories.

Can Earth Boy survive with Eclipso the Evil? Will there be enough sunlight in the world for both of them?

Booker hopped out of the car and headed up to Germ's house.

He had a new chapter to write.

(18)

My Best Friend

Booker stood on the front porch and knocked.

"Go away," came a voice from inside.

"Germ, it's me, Booker. Your friend."

"We're ex-friends. You dumped on my limericks, and you got me in trouble with Ox."

Booker didn't know what to say. "You're right. But I'm sorry. Can I come in?"

"No."

"What happened with Ox?"

The door cracked open one inch.

"I'd show you what his face looked like when I read him the limerick, but I can't, because you can't come in."

Through the one inch space in the door came the tempting smell of Mrs. Germondo's cooking. He remembered the oozing tuna casseroles and the dozens of pizzas and his stomach growled. "What's your mother making?"

"Nothing for you."

"Come on, Germ. I said I was sorry. You want me to get down on my knees and beg forgiveness?"

"No," Germ said.

"Just show me the face?"

The door opened a little more.

"You won't believe this," Germ said.

"Try me."

Germ stuck his head out of the crack in the door and made the face.

It was great—eyebrows arched, mouth in an *O*, nose pinched in.

Booker laughed. Germ laughed. The door opened and Germ came out onto the porch.

Eclipso the Evil moved out of the life-giving beams of the sun and Earth Boy felt the warmth of the rays on his face again. There was enough light for both of them. The war was over.

"Can I hear the limerick?" Booker asked Germ.

"Which one?"

"The one about Ox."

"I thought you didn't like limericks," Germ said.

"I changed my mind," said Booker. "They are actually pretty funny." He was surprised to admit this even to himself.

"Well," Germ said. "Actually I like science fiction stories, too."

Germ read some limericks and Booker listened. The more he listened the funnier they seemed.

"You want to read my new book?" Booker asked Germ.

Germ took the notebook. "This is so cool," he said as he turned the page.

Germ made a sound like the music before a scary movie, then read the title in a dramatic voice.

"Space Cat: Alone in Space!"

Booker smiled as Germ read the first chapter. The kitten was cowering in the corner afraid to begin a journey.

Booker was already thinking ahead to the happy ending he would write:

Lionardo and Felini stood and looked at the stars around them. Lionardo sighed a sigh of contentment. He had made a long journey. From a frightened kitten to a transformed super cat, from wanting total isolation to making the choice of action.

He was glad that he had taken the chance to save Felini. He had a new friend.

They didn't speak. No words were necessary. As the ship turned, a supernova swung into view.

The colors were incredible. Reds and yellows swirled in between blues and greens. They were struck with wonder.

"Thank you," Felini said.

Booker Jones
Pickle Springs, AR

October 10

Hamerstein Books
New York, NY

Dear Editor,

I was going to send you the rest of my book <u>Space Cat:
Alone in Space</u> but I've decided just to keep this one for myself. You might think that's a waste of time, writing a book
and deciding not to publish it, but no writing is ever wasted.
Everything we write teaches us something. That's what my
grandfather, Pop, taught me.

You can keep the first three chapters. And don't worry, I
haven't stopped writing, I'm just writing a new kind of chapter right now. That's what Pop calls working on relationships.

Do you realize that I have been sending you books and
you have been rejecting them for over a year now? It's a rela-
tionship!

Fur-ever Yours,
Booker Jones

P.S. What is your name?

Hamerstein Books
New York, NY

October 25

Booker Jones
Pickle Springs, AR

Dear Mr. Jones,

My name is George.

Sincerely,

George Watson

George Watson
Hamerstein Books

Betsy Duffey's novel *Utterly Yours, Booker Jones* was the recipient of several state awards as well as many other honors. The author of numerous books for young readers, she lives in Atlanta, Georgia, with her husband and two children.

*